SIEB POSTHUMA

TRANSLATED BY BILL NAGELKERKE

Where is RUSTY?

GECKO PRESS

Rusty, Henrietta, and Toby are going to town with Rusty's mother.
"The next stop is ours," says Mother. "Who wants to push the button?"

They get off at the department store.
Mother makes them wait outside the enormous doors.

"It's very busy inside," she says. "So what do we do?"
"We all stay together!" chant Rusty, Henrietta, and Toby.

"Look at everything!" says Toby. "There's a hair salon. Shall I get my coat curled?"
"Silly sausage," says Henrietta. "Your coat's much too short.
Let's go to the perfume counter instead. They might let us sniff things."

"Maybe later," says Mother. "First, we're going up the escalator."
Rusty's not listening. He's sniffing the air. Something smells delicious.

Rusty follows his nose.
He steps into the elevator. Before he knows it he's on the fourth floor, in homewares.

"Whipping up biscuits is a breeze; this smart machine won't fail to please!
No more mess! No more fuss! For picky guests and hungry pups,
this handy gadget is a must!" sings the lady behind the counter.

"Mother, we must get one of these!" says Rusty. He turns round.
"Mother?"
There's no sign of her, or Henrietta, or Toby.

Two watchdogs are on patrol.

"There are stray pups on the loose," says one.

"If we catch them we'll lock them in the pound!"

Rusty has to get away, fast.

Rusty flees through the ventilation pipes. It's dark down here! He runs and runs and runs. Strange sounds are everywhere: a drip from a water pipe,

the tick-tick of the central heating and, far off, the hum of the busy department store. At last he sees a light ahead. He makes sure the coast is clear before he scrambles out.

Where is he? There are boxes and parcels everywhere.

It must be the storeroom.

Rusty hears something. Someone's coming! Is it the watchdogs?

He scrambles into a box.

In the Lost Dogs department, Rusty's mother is in tears.
They make an announcement for her: "Attention, please. We have a missing dog.
A small white fox terrier with a red collar. His name is Rusty.
If you find him, please come to Lost Dogs on the third floor."

Down in the storeroom, Rusty doesn't hear a thing.
He stays hidden in the box as it's trundled through the store.

He wants to find his mother but he's terrified the watchdogs will see him.
Everyone in the department store is looking for Rusty.

They look between the cabinets and tables in the furniture department.
Where is Rusty?

They look among the soft toys in the toy department.
Where is Rusty?

They look among the mannequins in the clothing department.
Where is Rusty?

In the lighting department someone yelps, "That lamp just moved!"
The salesperson says, "I'm sure we don't have a lamp in our collection with hairy feet."

"A small dog has been found in the lighting department, sales desk 23,"
says a voice over the intercom.
All the dogs dash over, with Mother, Toby, and Henrietta leading the way.

"I'd know that wag anywhere," says Mother. "It's my own little Rusty!"

"Next time you must stay with me," she tells him once they're home safe and sound. But Rusty's not listening. He's worn out and dreaming about the dog-biscuit machine.